For Mum and for Pamella

ORCHARD BOOKS

First published in Great Britain in 2016 by The Watts Publishing Group

1 3 5 7 9 10 8 6 4 2

Text and illustrations copyright Fabi Santiago, 2016

The moral rights of the author have been asserted.

A CIP catalogue record for this book is available from the British Library.

ISBN 978 1 40833 688 5

Printed and bound in China

Orchard Books
An imprint of Hachette Children's Group
Part of The Watts Publishing Group Limited
Carmelite House
50 Victoria Embankment
London EC4Y 0DZ

An Hachette UK Company
www.hachette.co.uk

www.hachettechildrens.co.uk

FABI SANTIAGO

Tiger in a tutu

ORCHARD

Once upon a time in Paris, not so very
long ago, there lived a tiger called Max.

Max was no ordinary tiger . . .

he was a tiger with a dream.

balancé

pirouette

All he wanted in the world was

grand jeté

plié

pas de chat

to be a **ballet dancer!**

Every day, Max went to Ballet School.
Not to dance, for no tigers were allowed in
class. Instead, he gazed longingly through
the window, wishing he could join in.

Max had NO ballet shoes, NO tutu,
and only the music in his heart.

But still Max didn't give up.

He pirouetted . . .

. . . through the streets of Paris.

He leapt gracefully across the River Seine . . .

. . . and finally, lost in his dream, Max finished with a flourish and a twirl at the very tip . . .

. . . of the top of the Eiffel Tower.

But when Max
looked out, there was
NO audience,
NO applause.

Everyone had disappeared!
No one wanted a tiger
dancing through the
Paris streets.

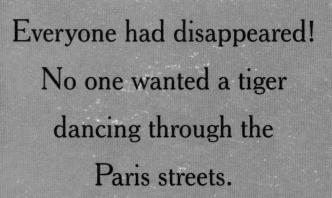

"My dream will never come true,"
said Max with a sigh.
"I will never shine on any stage."

But not *everyone* had disappeared.
One little ballerina had been
watching Max dance.
"*Bonjour!* I'm Celeste," she said.
"Wipe your tears and come with me.
I have a plan!"

Backstage at the ballet, Celeste helped Max get ready. She found him the perfect pair of ballet shoes . . .

. . . and a tiger-sized tutu.

"What if everyone runs away AGAIN?" Max worried. Celeste took his paw. "Pretend that you are pirouetting through Paris," she whispered.

"Dance like only you can dance. You are Max, the tiger in a tutu!"

So Max leapt
into the spotlight.
What a glorious entrance.
What a moment to shine.

What a . . .

. . . STAMPEDE!

When Max looked out, there was
NO audience, NO applause.
But this time, he was not alone.
He heard a little voice say,
"Let's dance – just us two."

So, together, Max and Celeste
pirouetted and pliéd.

They twirled . . .

they tippy-toed . . .

voilà!

. . . and they finished
with a beautiful curtsey.

Then Max and Celeste heard cheers.

They heard whoops and shouts!

They looked out and saw that the stampede had stopped. The audience had turned to watch the friends dance!

At last, Max's dream had come true.

He was a ballet star, shining on the stage!

And, best of all, now he had a
friend to dance by his side.

PARIS